Farah Rocks

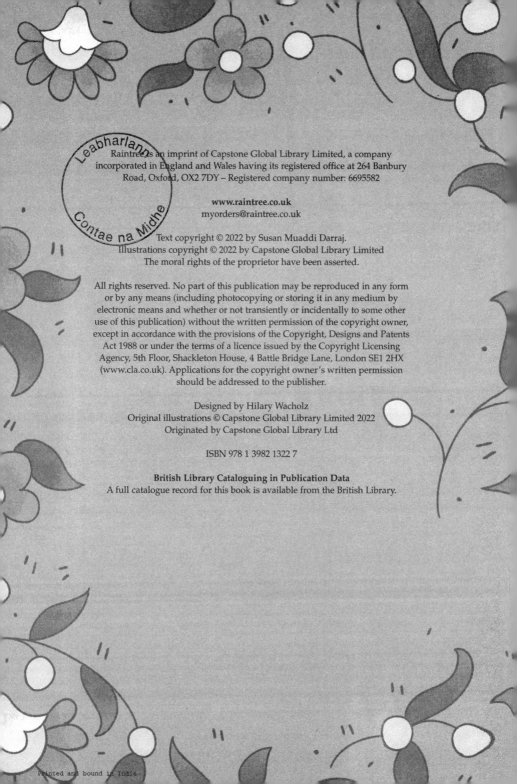

Raintree is an imprint of Capstone Global Library Limited, a company incorporated in England and Wales having its registered office at 264 Banbury Road, Oxford, OX2 7DY – Registered company number: 6695582

www.raintree.co.uk
myorders@raintree.co.uk

Text copyright © 2022 by Susan Muaddi Darraj.
Illustrations copyright © 2022 by Capstone Global Library Limited
The moral rights of the proprietor have been asserted.

Designed by Hilary Wacholz
Original illustrations © Capstone Global Library Limited 2022
Originated by Capstone Global Library Ltd

ISBN 978 1 3982 1322 7

British Library Cataloguing in Publication Data
A full catalogue record for this book is available from the British Library.

Printed and bound in India

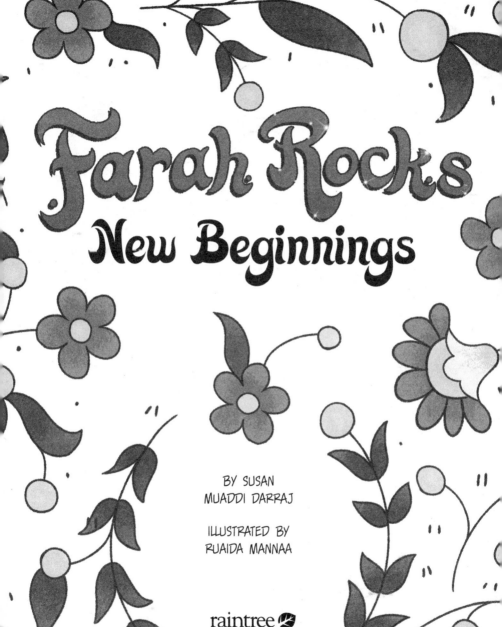

Farah Rocks
New Beginnings

BY SUSAN
MUADDI DARRAJ

ILLUSTRATED BY
RUAIDA MANNAA

raintree 🦋

a Capstone company — publishers for children

CHAPTER 1

"Farah, keep walking. We don't want to be left behind," Mama says as she gently pushes my back.

I'm in front of the Einstein Academy's library, a brick building filled with thousands of books. My old school's one-room library was near the music classes. My reading was always interrupted by flute practice or tuba lessons.

"Our library is just one of the things that makes Einstein Academy so remarkable," says the assistant head, Ms Maxim, who is leading the tour. A group of parents and students, including me and my mama and baba, are here for a school visit. "We have more than ten thousand volumes, plus more than forty databases of articles and e-books."

Here's the truth: Ms Maxim looks like the most unbookish person I've ever met. She is wearing a crisp black suit with high heels and more make-up than a magazine model. She looks like she belongs in an office in a big city, signing important papers and shouting, "Get the president on the phone!"

But ten thousand books? I'm float-walking now. I love to read so much that sometimes I forget to eat. On the way here, I read my new mythology book and almost didn't realize the fifteen-minute drive was over because Athena had been about to destroy the Trojans. I love to read so much that lately I've even started writing my own stories.

"Let's move on," says Ms Maxim. The cluster of new students and parents obey her like puppies.

"Can we see the inside of the library first?" I ask.

Allie Liu, my Official Best Friend, giggles next to me. She probably knew I'd ask that question. She knows everything I'm thinking. (She should, of course. We've been Official Best Friends for years.)

Ms Maxim looks at me and holds up a clipboard. "Your name?"

"Farah Hajjar."

"Hee-jar?" she tries.

"You can just call me Farah Rocks," I say helpfully.

"Now why would I do that?" she asks.

"Well, *Hajjar* means 'rocks' in Arabic," I explain. Everyone's called me that since nursery school.

"I'll use your actual name," she says. She smiles at me like a plastic doll, and I know it's only because my mum is standing right behind me.

"There will be time later, Ms Hajjar," she tells me. "Now, on to the science labs."

"Well, you said you were proud of the library," I start to protest. I'm not trying to be difficult, but it would take, like, two minutes to see the inside. Just a quick look. But Mama nudges me with her finger and whispers, "Imshee."

Ms Maxim is ignoring me anyway, so I follow the group, dragging my feet.

"Nobody is at Einstein for the books," says a voice behind me. "Every school has books. Not every school has science labs."

I turn round so quickly that the person who owns the voice slams into me. I see a body wearing jeans and a brown flannel shirt, but no face – just a bush of green hair, like a tree.

"Hey!" says the Tree. Both hands come up to make a triangle opening in the hair. I see one brown eye like a cyclops, glaring at me.

Holy hummus.

"Well, *I* wanted to see the library," I say uncertainly, because I've never talked to a tree before.

"Waste of time," says the Tree, hurrying around me to catch up with Ms Maxim's clicking heels.

"Come on, girls," say Mama and Mrs Liu, pushing forwards.

Allie and I roll our eyes. Our mothers are actually more excited about the Einstein Academy than we are.

The Einstein Academy is a school for "gifted" kids. Teachers have called us "gifted", although the only "gift" we seem to get is more homework than anyone else.

"Who is that kid?" I ask Allie as we trot after everyone else. "The one with the green hair?"

"Bryan Najjarian," she says, like a reporter. "Also in our year. Attended Highlandtown Charter School."

"And . . . the green hair?"

"You didn't notice it before in assembly?" she asks as we follow our group into the science building. "Pretty hard to miss green hair."

I shrug and wave to Mama, who has paused to see where I am.

"Oh, Farah," she whispers, grabbing my hand in excitement. "This place is so amazing. What a lucky girl you are!"

Ahead of us, standing in front of a row of Bunsen burners, is the Tree. He turns, parts his hair and smirks at me.

CHAPTER 2

On Saturday, Mama asks me to stay with Samir because Baba works and she needs to shop for school supplies. This year, because I'm starting at Einstein Academy, I need special items, like graph paper, a fancy calculator and pencils in certain colours.

Samir is excited, he says, to "stay with Faw-wah". That's what he calls me because he can't pronounce his *R*s. His speech therapist says that eventually he will. At the moment, he has a loose tooth as well.

Today is also his sixth birthday, and Mama has baked him a cake, which we'll have later tonight.

"I'm worried about my toof!" he tells Mama as she

carefully smooths white icing on the cake with the back of a spoon.

"Samir, I used a *special batter* for this cake, and it won't hurt your tooth," Mama tells him soothingly.

"A *special* battah?" Now he's thrilled. "What's in it?"

"A secret ingredient from the tooth fairy." Mama kisses his forehead. "Okay, back soon. Samir, listen to Farah."

She empties her purse, throwing out old receipts and papers in the bin.

"Farah, please make him a sandwich in an hour – turkey and cheese are in the fridge. Baba will be home around noon, so you can all eat lunch together."

"By the way," I tell her, as I watch her slide her feet into her shoes, "I'll probably get loads more homework now. I might not have time for babysitting or chores."

"You know," Mama says, pausing with her hand on the doorknob, "that I have six younger brothers and sisters? And that I was changing nappies when I was only seven years old? And washing dirty laundry by hand in a big tub when I was only eight?" She blows a kiss to Samir and me. "Remind me to tell you those stories tonight, in lots of detail."

I groan.

She laughs as she strides out to the car. As I shut the door behind her, I hear the bottom panel jiggle, and I readjust the duct tape that is holding it together. Our door has been broken for years, but Mama and Baba are waiting until it gets really bad before replacing it.

Mama is worried about how much that calculator will cost, although she won't tell me that. She did tell me that she searched online last night for a used one but had no luck.

"What should we do, Samir?" I ask my brother. "We have two whole hours to ourselves."

"Eat cake!" he says brightly, examining his loose tooth in the hallway mirror.

"That's for tonight," I remind him. "We're going to sing 'Happy Birthday' to you – me, Mama and Baba." I start singing it for him, in English and then Arabic:

"*Sana hilweh, ya gameel! Sana hilweh, ya Samiiiiiiirrrrrrr!*" I exaggerate my voice like an opera singer, and he bursts out laughing.

"Again! With a candle!" he says, running to the kitchen. "Please, Faw-wah!"

"No, tonight," I tell him again, but he won't give up. He yanks on the drawer handle beside the sink, which is where Mama keeps a supply of old birthday candles and matches (which is why there's a safety lock on it).

"Fine, fine," I say. I unlatch the drawer. "But our secret, okay?"

He is shining like a candle himself, so excited that he starts jumping up and down on the tiled floor.

"Calm down," I urge him as I pull out a single blue candle, stick it in the cake, and light the match. I make him hurry before the candle drips wax onto the cake. He closes his eyes, makes a wish, and puffs out the flame.

"Well done!" I throw the candle and

match in the bin, then I smooth over the hole in the icing with a spoon. "I hope you made a good wish."

"I did! Do you want to know it, Faw-wah?"

"Nope. Keep it a secret. That's the rule."

A few minutes later, we decide to play football in our garden. Our garden is about the size of four car parking spaces. But we set up a goal at either end. I let Samir kick the ball into my goal (which really is a pedal bin turned on its side). He's thrilled, and I like to see him jump up and shout "Aw-wight!"

We're having so much fun that I don't hear our neighbour, Mrs Glover, who is working in her garden. She waves her hands at me and shouts over the fence, "Farah, dear, do you hear that?"

I stop, hugging the football to my chest. She freezes too, her gardening spade in the air as we listen. It's a shrill sound, but far away. She shrugs and so do I, and Samir and I continue our game.

Fifteen minutes later, just as I am about to ask Samir if he wants to eat anything, three things happen at once:

1. I hear Baba screaming our names, "Farah! Samir!" in a ghost-scary way.

2. Mrs Glover starts shouting at me and Samir to climb over the fence into her garden.

3. I smell smoke.

"They're here, Mr Hajjar! Out here!" Mrs Glover is shouting. "Frank!" She shouts at her husband, who appears at their back door with a phone to his ear.

"I'm calling emergency services. Is anyone in your house?" he asks me grimly, and I shake my head no.

Mrs Glover has finally got Baba's attention. He runs around the side of the house and jumps over her fence in one leap. His hands, face and clothes are blackened by soot. He kneels down and pulls me and Samir into his arms. I can smell smoke on his shirt.

I look over his shoulder at our house and see orange flames leaping behind the kitchen window.

Then I hear a pop. The kitchen window has shattered.

"Holy hummus!" I shriek. "Our house is on fire!"

CHAPTER 3

In the end, it takes three fire engines to visit Hollow Woods Lane and douse the fire in our kitchen. Samir and I watch from across the street as the firefighters rush into our house with hoses.

Baba calls Mama, and when she arrives, she and Baba keep their arms around us the whole time, squeezing our shoulders every once in a while. It's like they're reminding themselves that we are okay.

When the fire is out, the firefighters open all the windows. We watch as black smoke streams out of every window in our house, rising up into the sky like a storm cloud.

When the smoke clears, I gaze at our home. Most of the windows are broken, and the black soot that lines the window's edges look like smudged mascara. It's a terrible sight.

Mama and Baba need to stay with the firefighters and the police, so the Lius pick up Samir and me and take us to their house. They hug us, give us juice and feed us peanut butter and jam sandwiches. While we eat, Mr and Mrs Liu sit at their kitchen table, talking in worried voices and texting my mum.

Allie's older brother, Timothy, is usually a pain. But maybe because Samir and I look scared, he offers to watch *Tommy Turtle* with my brother while Allie and I go up to her room.

"What caused it?" she asks, stretched out on her pink rug, twisting her fingers through her black hair. She always does that when she's nervous.

"Beats me," I say, lying down on her bed. My heart is beating pretty hard, but at the same time, I feel numb. One minute, we're playing football, and the next, our house looks like a campfire. "You know what?" I tell Allie. "I just realized that my dad must have been terrified. He said he came home early, saw the flames and ran inside looking for us!"

"He could have been hurt!" she says. "Imagine if you really had been inside, trapped upstairs and –"

"Stop!" I clap my hands over my ears. "It's freaking me out."

"I'm sorry, Farah," she says and gives me a big hug. "What a disaster. And school starts on Tuesday!"

. . .

Later, Mama and Baba arrive at the Lius' home, looking exhausted. Mama's face looks as worn as an ancient scroll. They both smell of smoke, and Baba's clothes are still black with soot. They have a plastic bag, filled with T-shirts and joggers. All our clothes are ruined, they tell me, so they've bought a few things to get us through the weekend.

"Don't worry about your rock collection, Farah,"

Baba says. "Your books are ruined, but your rocks are fine."

Mama whispers to me, "You know Samir's favourite trainers?"

"His Tommy Turtle ones? The ones that say 'Kapow!'?"

She nods with a sigh. "Don't tell him, but now they're kaput."

Mrs Liu insists my parents shower while she cooks dinner for everyone. An hour later, Samir and Timothy are eating on the patio, but the rest of us sit at the table and hear Baba's update.

"The kitchen is destroyed, and the living room," he explains with a sigh, "blus two bedrooms ubstairs have major damage. The rest of the house is okay, but it's filled with smoke, so everything has to go – the sofas, the mattresses, the clothes, the carbets. All of it."

Allie smiles at me. She loves the way my dad talks. Because there is no *P* or *V* in Arabic, Baba replaces them with *B*s. But I'm too upset to smile back. All our stuff is ruined!

"The insurance company said they would replace all of it," Mama adds, patting my hand when she sees my face. "But it will take time. We have to live somewhere else until they fix it all."

"But how did it start?" Mr Liu asks as he walks around, pouring water in everyone's glass.

"They don't know," Mama replies. She's not eating her food, just moving the rice and chicken around on her plate. "Something in the kitchen. They don't think it was electrical. I'm just . . ."

We all stop and stare at her. Her face looks like she's just awakened from a nightmare, and her usually thick hair, damp from the shower, clings to the side of her face. ". . . I'm just in shock!" she finishes.

I wonder if that's the feeling I had earlier while lying on Allie's bed – that scared feeling when I couldn't get my heart to beat normally.

Shock. What an excellent word.

"It's a puzzle," Mama says. "It started in the back corner of the kitchen, but how?"

"Are any appliances there?" asks Mrs Liu.

"Nothing's there – just the rubbish bin."

A thought starts swimming around in my brain like a mermaid trying to break through the water. I can't quite understand what I'm supposed to remember, or do or say.

"The children are safe," Baba says, "and we are safe. Nothing else matters."

The Lius nod their agreement.

Samir comes in with his empty plate just then. "Yummy!" he tells Mrs Liu. "Thank you!"

"You're welcome. By the way, Samir," she says, "is it true that today is your birthday?"

"Yeah!" he says. "I'm six!"

Mama grins. "Samir," she says, "nothing – not even a house fire – could make us forget your birthday, habibi." She winks at Baba. "Abdallah, go and get it."

"I'll be right back," Baba says grandly and stands up. "Don't go anywhere, habibi."

A minute later, he comes back with a cake from the bakery, decorated with white icing and blue writing that says, *Happy 6th Birthday, Samir!*

My brother shrieks in delight.

Mrs Liu lights a candle, and we all sing "Happy Birthday". I sing it again, in Arabic, with my parents, and then the Lius surprise us and break into Mandarin, singing, *"Zhù ni shengrì kuàilè."*

"Make a wish!" we urge him. Samir screws his eyes shut and then blows out the candle.

While Mama cuts the cake, I notice Mr Liu take the candle and the matchstick to the sink and run water on them before throwing them in the bin.

And the mermaid in my mind breaks through the surface.

CHAPTER 4

At Sunday mass, Father Alexander makes a big speech about our house and how the parish will pray for us.

In the pew between my parents, I feel sick, like I've swallowed a rock. *Here's the truth,* I think. *I started a fire and ruined our house.*

During coffee hour, several people stop by to ask us what we need. They're all very nice, except I really don't want Mrs Hassan's granddaughter's old chest of drawers or Mr Diwan's daughter's old winter coat.

Mama goes to the snack table to get Samir some milk and returns looking annoyed. Baba touches her elbow, his secret way of asking what's wrong. She tilts her head towards the queue for coffee, where Mrs Khoury stands.

You can see Mrs Khoury's lipstick from the next town. She also always wears brightly coloured dresses with heels so high that I worry about her safety when she hobbles up to get Communion.

Her daughter Lana is there too. Her clothes are so expensive that I'm sure her coat costs more than Mama's old car. She's also very mean. Over the summer, Lana stole flyers I'd posted all over Harbourtown to promote my tutoring business.

"What's wrong?" Baba asks Mama.

"She's heading over here," Mama whispers.

Sure enough, Mrs Khoury and Lana walk over to us, both smelling of heavy perfume that makes me want to sneeze.

As Mrs Khoury talks to my parents, making *tsk*-ing noises as she asks about the fire, Lana looks at me and says, "Well, you never had nice clothes to begin with. It may not be a bad thing that they all burned."

. • .

Later that day, the insurance agent meets my parents and me at Hollow Woods Lane to see if anything can be saved. Samir stays with the Lius but begs me to find his Tommy Turtle trainers. My stomach aches, because I know they're ruined.

"No family film night tonight," Baba says in the car, "but Samir will understand."

I wonder if Baba will understand when he finds out that it was my fault the fire started. We stayed at the Lius' house last night, but I barely slept. I woke up and used the light coming from the hallway to write a little story. In my story, a girl plays outside while her house burns behind her. It's not fiction. It's an autobiography.

As we drive up to our house, I notice the front door has been boarded up with a brown wooden plank, like someone taped a giant plaster over our home. "I was scared," Baba explains. "I saw fire and thought you were inside. I couldn't get my key in the lock, so I just kicked it open."

"Well, we can get that new door now, right?" I joke, but no one laughs.

We wear white masks on our faces to cover our noses and mouths when we enter. Our living room and kitchen look like a black-and-white film, everything covered with soot and ash. I feel like Persephone arriving in the underworld after being kidnapped by Hades.

Mama looks like she's about to cry. *If she does*, I think, *I will probably also sob like a baby.*

Baba hugs Mama. "We are safe. Remember what's important."

The insurance agent wears a white cap with the name of the company on it. She says she's sorry for our misfortune, but adds, "We'll get it sorted out."

Handing us each black plastic sacks, she tells us to take anything that can be saved. Mama and Baba have already taken Mama's jewellery box, a load of photos and Samir's medicines.

"If something is damaged," the agent says, handing us each a clipboard, "write it down."

Then she tells us it'll take three months to repair everything. My parents gasp, and my stomach aches.

"The floors and walls are smoke-damaged, so they all need replacing. The kitchen and living room need a complete rebuild," she explains. "So." She checks a paper in her file. "We're going to place you in a house, not a hotel, until it's finished."

"Do you know yet how it started?" Mama asks.

I look worriedly at the woman, but she shakes her head no. "That will take more time," she says.

I'm lying. I'm not saying anything that's not true, but not saying anything at all is also a form of lying. I know that. But for now, I am relieved.

As we go through the house with clipboards and black sacks, I find my rock collection. It's mostly chunks that Baba brings home from the quarry, where he cuts stone. It's what his father did too – that's how we got the name *Hajjar*.

The books on my shelf are ruined, like Baba said. But I dig under my mattress and find my book on rocks and minerals and my big book of Greek mythology. They're both fine, even though my bed and pillows are grey with ash.

Some of the clothes in my chest of drawers are fine, though Mama says they'll have to be taken to the dry cleaners in case. The clothes hanging in my wardrobe are covered in a thick layer of soot. The insurance agent tells us to just throw them out. "That residue is tough to remove," she tells Mama. "Also, almost everything in your son's room needs to be thrown out."

In the hallway, I see Samir's Tommy Turtle trainers sticking out of a box labelled *Rubbish*. It seems really unfair to me that I'm the only one whose favourite things were saved.

I remove my mask, because a tear trickles down my nose, but the air is so dirty that I quickly put it back on.

CHAPTER 5

Back at the Lius, Samir actually seems excited that we're moving to a new house.

"It's just for a short while," Baba explains when he starts bouncing up and down.

"But Faw-wah, that was my wish! A new house!" When I don't reply, he adds, "Wemembah my wish?"

"Oh, when he blew out his candles the other night," Allie says, laughing.

Samir stops bouncing. I know he's about to say something, like, *"No, the wish I made yesterday when Faw-wah lit the candle for me and sang in her funny voice."*

Just as I think of how to distract him, he shrieks and

yells, "My toof!" The tooth that has bothered him all week sits in his palm. There is a gaping hole in his smile.

Everyone makes a big deal about the tooth, which gives me a chance to sneak up to Allie's room to think. I feel as guilty as a criminal.

Allie finds me lying on her rug later and hands me a juice carton. "It's almost Tuesday," she says.

"What's Tuesday?" A panic spreads through me.

She stares at me. "We start school on Tuesday."

"Oh, right." I sip my juice.

"You know," Allie says, "I heard my mum saying that your parents have okay insurance so you guys should be fine. It's not going to . . . you know . . ."

"Make us even more poor?"

Allie sighs. "You're not poor, Farah Rocks."

I know that we're not sleeping-in-the-train-station poor. But my mum's car makes a chugging noise every time she puts it in gear. And the soles on Baba's work shoes are paper-thin. And what do I do to help out?

I go and burn down the house.

I feel so bad about the whole thing that I can't stop thinking about it. There's a story in Greek mythology about Cronus, who had a bad habit of eating his kids. When his wife had another baby, Zeus, she hid him and fed Cronus a rock disguised as a child. Well, it's like I swallowed a rock too, except this one is getting bigger and bigger, weighing me down.

. . .

The insurance agent is like a fairy godmother. She ticks stuff on her clipboard and it just happens. She tells us we will spend a few nights in a hotel until the rental house is ready. We thank the Lius and drive to the Harbourtown Hotel.

In the room, Mama pulls me aside and hands me a plastic bag. "You need these for school tomorrow."

"Thanks, Mama," I say as I open the bag. There's the calculator, pencils, a compass, folders and notebooks.

There's something else: a small red notebook with a fabric cover and pockets on the inside.

"Something special for you," she whispers. "Maybe you can write down what you're thinking while we're dealing with . . . with everything."

I thank her, feeling more guilty than ever. The only time I can forget that feeling is when I'm writing stories about it. In my stories, the fire is happening to someone else, another girl, not me. In my stories, the person who started the fire is a fictional girl, not Farah Hajjar.

Samir and I share one of the queen-sized beds. I pull the blue sheets around us and cuddle him.

"Why is evewyone so sad?" he whispers to me.

"Nobody is sad," I tell him, then change the subject. "Pretty soon, we'll see our new house."

"Get some sleep, my darlings," Mama mumbles from the next bed. Baba is already snoring.

"Faw-wah, can you believe my wish came twue?" Samir whispers. "I have a secwet powah."

No, I think. *You just have a terrible sister.*

CHAPTER 6

Mama drops Allie and me off at Einstein Academy on Tuesday. She parks in the drop-off line and gets out of the car. As I hoist my backpack over my shoulder, Mama leans down so close that I can smell her coconut shampoo. "Is it okay if I hug you?" she asks seriously.

I look around. Kids are streaming from the car park to the front doors of the school.

"I'm gonna say no," I tell her honestly. "Sorry."

"No problem," she says and sticks out her hand. "Is this okay?"

We shake hands formally, like we just signed a business deal, and we both crack up. So does Allie.

"I'm proud of you, Farah. You too, Allie," Mama says, before driving away.

There are black and red balloons lining the path up to the doors, and I feel excited and nervous all at once.

Allie and I are in the same classroom. The door of room twenty-two is decorated like a science experiment. There is a picture of a huge beaker made out of coloured paper that covers the entire door except for the knob. Inside the beaker is a bubbly liquid. When we look closer, we see that the bubbles are actually tiny photographs of all the new students.

"There we are!" says Allie, pointing to the middle of the beaker. "Oh, and there's that boy."

The Tree. Even in his official school photo, you can only see one eye poking out from behind his hair.

"What is up with the green hair?" I say. "He looks so weird. I mean, who does that?"

"Well, I have green hair because . . . ," says a voice from behind me.

Holy hummus.

I turn around, and the Tree pauses, shaking the curls out of his eyes. ". . . I am original," he says. Then he opens the door and enters room twenty-two, letting it slam behind him.

"Rude," I stammer. But I feel bad for calling him weird.

As soon as we walk in, we see a man standing at the front of the class, wearing a red shirt and jeans. He's juggling three tennis balls in the air.

"Hurry up! Everyone find a seat!" he shouts at us. "Not sure how long I can keep this going."

The only two empty seats next to one another are in the back, right behind the Tree.

"So! I'm Mr Beaker," says the man loudly. "When I throw you a ball, catch it, then tell me your name and one cool fact about yourself. Got it?"

We all nod. The Tree's curls bounce in front of me like the wind blowing through the leaves on a branch.

"Good. GO!"

Mr Beaker stops juggling and, lightning quick, tosses a ball to a thin boy with glasses in the front row.

"Ummm . . . should I stand?" the boy asks.

"Yes!" replies Mr Beaker.

"Okay, well, I'm Rajesh Gupta," says the boy, rising. "And . . . something cool? I speak Urdu and I read Latin."

"Awesome, Rajesh!" Mr Beaker throws the second ball to a tall girl in the third row, who has long, curly blond hair.

"My name is Amanda Cook," she says, speaking confidently, "and I actually love to cook!" Everyone laughs. "I make the best blueberry waffles ever," she declares. Someone hoots.

"Next!" Mr Beaker says, throwing the ball to Allie, who stands up too.

"Allie Liu," she says matter-of-factly. "I like to play chess."

As more and more kids get called, I try hard to think of a cool fact.

Why don't you mention how you just burned down your family's house? says a little voice in my head. My stomach begins to ache.

Then I hear a voice I recognize: "Winston Suarez." I look up in surprise. Winston is a friend from my old school. I never even saw him in the room. Guess I'd been distracted by the Tree and the juggling.

"I have severe allergies to thirty-two known substances," he says as he stands up, "including peanuts, kiwi and chickpeas."

"Glad to know that!" says Mr Beaker, who then throws the ball to a slender girl in denim overalls. She has thick black hair in long plaited pigtails.

"I'm June Jordan Williams," she says quietly. "My mum named me after a famous poet."

"Good stuff! Look out!" he calls out. Too late, I realize he's talking to me.

The tennis ball hits me right in the middle of my forehead. I have no time to block it because my arms are wrapped around my stomach. "Ooof!" I cry out.

"You okay, young lady?" asks Mr Beaker. "Sorry about that. By the end of the year, you'll be catching all my throws," he promises. "Now." He bounces the two balls he's still holding and catches them. "Name?"

"Farah Hajjar," I say, standing up.

"Cool fact?" he prompts me.

"I like rocks," I say.

"Rocks? Hmm . . . okay!" Mr Beaker throws the ball to the next person, who actually catches it.

"I mean, I collect them," I say, but he's already moved on.

"Was my answer weird?" I whisper to Allie as I sit back down.

Before she can answer, the Tree turns round and whispers, "Totally weird."

CHAPTER 7

Later that morning, Mr Beaker hands out sheets with our timetables. Just before dismissal, from 2:40 to 3:15, is something called Club Time.

Mr Beaker tells us that Einstein pupils must take part in one club every term. "Later this week, the older students will invite you to a Club Fair to show you the options."

How cool, I think, *that clubs are part of our school-work here*. Harbourtown had some clubs, like drama or netball, but they happened after school. I hope there's a geology club or a story-writing club. Maybe a language club, where I can learn Spanish.

Mr Beaker holds up fat felt pens and tells us to write our names across the top of our desks.

I have never had a teacher ask me to write on my desk. I'm top-of-the-roller-coaster thrilled.

He hands out felt pens like sweets. "When you've finished, go and find a locker you like, and write your name on that too."

I can't believe we're allowed to pick our own lockers. Allie and I pick ones next to each other, of course. Next to me, Rajesh draws a mini-solar system under his name on his locker. It takes him about a minute, but it's perfect. There's the sun, eight planets, and one dwarf planet. Earth even has little continents on its surface.

"Cool!" I tell Rajesh, who offers to draw something for me tomorrow.

Winston picks a locker down the corridor, close to the toilets. I see Enrique LeBrand, another friend from Harbourtown, and wave at him. He's in the other class, and they are also picking lockers.

The Tree, I notice, writes his name in green on the locker he's picked at the end of the corridor.

. . .

Even the canteen at Einstein is amazing. There are round tables set up all over the room, and there are more tables set up on an outdoor patio.

"Get your food and sit anywhere," Mr Beaker calls out to us.

My lunch bag was destroyed in the fire, so I get in the queue to buy food. The queue is long, but the cashier moves fast, ringing up everyone's lunch and welcoming them to Einstein. She wears a purple velvet cap decorated with gold braiding, and a badge that says, *We know what we are but know not what we may be.*

She sees me looking at it as she rings up my tray. "That's a quote from William Shakespeare. I wear a different one every day. I'm Mrs Salvatore, by the way," she says, taking my money.

"Farah Rocks."

"Welcome to Einstein, Farah Rocks."

Allie and I sit outside on the patio.

"This place is amazing," Allie says, opening her lunch box and looking round. "Our teacher juggles, we can eat lunch outside and everyone seems really nice. Well, almost everyone."

I see the Tree sitting by himself on a ledge that runs round the patio area. He eats a sandwich out of a small plastic bag and some pretzels out of another. I feel guilty for what I said about him this morning, but then shrug off the thought. He'd been rude to me since our school visit. If he wants to be alone, then he can be alone.

. . .

Almost every single subject is fun. In science, Mr Beaker takes us to a real laboratory, and we all put on white lab coats. And goggles – we each get our own pair. We pour, mix and boil liquids. He takes one of his tennis balls and dips it in liquid nitrogen, then smashes it against the table.

The only part of the day that doesn't one-hundred-per cent thrill me is Language Arts. The teacher, Ms Toste, wears sweatpants, a sweatshirt and running shoes. She rushes around the room, handing out books like they're on fire. They are biographies of famous people because we're going to be writing a book review, she explains.

I get a book about Marie Curie, a famous scientist.

"Finish reading, then we'll learn how to summarize," Ms Toste says. "At the Einstein Academy, we read for information."

Then she picks up a plastic model of a brain from her desk. "When you read," she continues, "you give your brain an amazing workout! Your brain loves to exercise."

And just then, she drops to the ground and does ten push-ups – with one hand.

Holy hummus.

We all stand up to watch. "Whoa!" whispers Enrique, who's a star athlete. "She's not even sweating."

When she finishes, Ms Toste hops back up and punches the air in triumph. "I feel good!" she announces. "And that's how my brain feels after reading."

I raise my hand then, and Ms Toste consults her list. "You're Farah . . . Hajjar?"

"Just call her Farah Rocks," offers Enrique helpfully. "Everyone does."

Before she can ask why, I get to my question: "I just wondered if we were going to write any stories or maybe poems in this class?"

"Stories? Poems?" she asks, as if I'd asked if we'd be learning how to cook pasta. "We'll do a little bit, yes." She walks up to me. I wonder if she will order me to do ten push-ups. "But you know what's a great story? The life of Marie Curie," she says, picking up my book and showing it to the class.

Then she tells us all to start reading.

From across the room, June Jordan smiles at me and shrugs her shoulders.

The Tree sneers – yes, sneers – at me.

CHAPTER 8

Baba joins us as we all drive to look at the new house. "Thirty-two L Street," says Baba, reading from a paper as Mama drives. "That's behind the funeral home."

"I don't want to live near a funeral home!" I exclaim.

Of course Samir, who's been quietly playing with a "Good Behaviour" sticker on his shirt, asks, "What's that, Faw-wah?"

"Nothing, habibi," Mama tells him and glares at me in the rearview mirror. I know when her eyebrows shoot up like that it means I'd better, as Baba says, "zib my lib".

So I do. Even though I have so many big questions.

Like, why doesn't our street have a proper name? Why would someone not give a street a full name? Did they run out of names or just get lazy?

"I thought the house would be on Seacrest," Mama mutters to Baba. "That's what the woman told us, no?"

"I guess she couldn't get that house," he replies.

"I hate this stweet! I don't like the lettah *L!*" Samir whines.

Mama sighs. "I still cannot believe this is all happening."

Baba turns around and talks to us, but I can tell he's really talking to Mama. "We are all safe," he says firmly. "Like I keeb telling you, nothing else matters. If we have to live in a tent, it is okay, because we are healthy and safe."

I think it would be more fair if, for two months, my family gets a nice, pretty house on Seacrest, and I get to live in a tent. I can imagine the insurance agent just ticking it off on her magic clipboard: "One leaky tent for a terrible person. Got it."

Mama turns right into a little development of townhouses behind the old train station. The houses are all much smaller than our house, and they all look the same: beige with brown doors. To me, they look like stained teeth.

We pass J and K Streets and finally get to L Street, and Baba reads the numbers off the homes until we find number thirty-two. It looks like all the others, sitting in the middle of a row of houses, which surround a green square of grass. In the middle of the square is a small bed of flowers, a bench and a football net.

I sit up and pay attention, because there is someone kicking a football into that net. Someone with green hair.

Holy hummus.

I sink down below the level of the window.

"Funny, Faw-wah," says Samir, unclipping his seat belt and sliding down as well. "Hide and seek?"

Mama parks and snaps at me: "Farah, *khalas!*" Enough.

But I'm in too much shock to listen. My parents both get out of the car and walk up to the front door.

Samir tugs on my arm. I peek out of the window and don't see the Tree, so I unbuckle my seat belt and open the door. But when I step out onto the pavement, he's right there in front of me.

"Hello there, Farah Rocks," he says, looking like he's about to laugh.

"Umm . . . hello," I mumble. What is he doing here?

"Who is this, Farah?" Baba asks. I can tell he is staring, as I knew he would, right at the Tree's head.

"I'm Bryan Najjarian," he introduces himself to my parents, and he even shakes their hands like a grown-up. Suddenly, his hair is pushed out of the way. For the first time, I can see both of his eyes at once. "Farah is in my class at Einstein."

"Can I see that?" Samir asks, and the Tree hands him the football.

"We can play later, if you like," he offers. Samir starts bouncing up and down.

"Yes, I remember you from our school visit," Mama tells the Tree. I can tell she likes him because she assumes he's clever. "Do you live here?"

"Yes, at number forty-eight, across the quad, with my dad."

"Why? What happened to your house?" I ask.

He glares at me for a second. "Nothing. That's where I *live*."

"Oh," I say. "Sorry."

"Bryan, ask your father if he'd like to come to our blace later, when he gets home from work," Baba says.

"Oh, he's already home," says the Tree. "He . . . uh . . . works a night shift, so he sleeps in the afternoon. So maybe later this week."

My parents wave goodbye, and he walks away, bouncing the ball on his knee. As Mama unlocks the front door, she says it would be nice to meet the neighbours, like the Tree's father.

"Yes," says Baba, laughing. Then he winks at me. "Maybe his hair is burble!"

I crack up laughing when he says that. But as we walk in through the front door, the laughter dies in my throat.

CHAPTER 9

There is beige everywhere. Everything – the walls, the floors, the wood trim around the windows, the kitchen worktop, the fridge – is beige. I open the kitchen cabinets, and the shelves inside are beige. I peek into the small bathroom, and the floors, the sink and yes, the toilet, are beige.

Our house on Hollow Woods Lane had been filled with colour, every room a different tone. Our dining room was red, our TV room was blue, our kitchen was yellow. Now I am in the beige underworld.

It is smaller than our own house, if that is possible. There isn't even room for a table in the kitchen.

The dining room has a small table in the corner. It's attached to the wall, with one leg holding up the other end. The table is made of beige plastic.

The living room has a small beige sofa and a big, soft beige chair. There is a small coffee table and curtains covering the back window of the house. All beige.

Samir and I run upstairs. There are three bedrooms with small beds, beige blankets and sheets, and small nightstands with beige lamps. Samir seems excited and picks the room in the middle. I put my backpack down on the bed in the back room, the smallest one.

I see Baba reach out and rub Mama's shoulder and say, "It's okay." And she nods and answers, "Yes, of course," like she is trying to convince herself.

I deserve a wardrobe instead of a room, I tell myself. *I should probably volunteer to sleep on the roof.*

The thing is, I know I have to tell my parents the truth. I wrote a story yesterday in which the girl who started a fire confessed everything. But it's easier to write a story about that than to actually do it in real life.

Baba and Mama make three trips to bring the few boxes of things we saved from the fire. In one box, Samir and I find four plastic pumpkins, which we always put outside of our house in the autumn. We arrange them now on the front step of this new house. I'm standing on the pavement, making sure they are lined up in the right order, biggest to smallest, when I hear a *thwack*. It's the Tree, practising his football kicks in the middle of the quad.

He looks up and catches my eye, and we stare at each other. Near by, I see some kids riding round on their bikes, shouting and yelling. The Tree sees them, takes his football, and goes inside his house.

. . .

Later that night, Mama attempts to cook in our new kitchen using some pans she borrowed from Mrs Liu. Somehow, while we put away clothes and hang some pictures up, Mama is able to whip up a pot of lentil soup and a tray of chicken and potatoes.

"Need some help?" I ask her, walking into the kitchen. I realize that there isn't really enough room for both of us. If Baba wanted to come in, one of us would have to leave.

"No, I'm almost there," Mama says, adjusting the temperature on the oven. "Did you put your clothes away?"

"Yep."

"You should have five sets of clothes for school," she says. "I think the church is doing an appeal for us, so we might have more next week."

"An appeal?"

"Yes, I told Father Alexander that most of our clothes were ruined. He said he would ask people to donate some."

"I don't want someone's used clothes!" I protest, feeling like the Tree just kicked his football right into my guts.

"Why not?" she asks, looking surprised. "People want to help."

"I'm not wearing used clothes," I say again.

"Farah, habibti," she says, pausing to lean against the worktop and stare at me. "When your father and I were growing up, we were happy to have anything that didn't have holes in it. I think you should be more grateful."

My heart hammers so hard that I wonder how my chest doesn't explode.

Mama pulls me into a hug. "Oh, habibti. I know this is all very upsetting for you. I promise you that soon we will be back home. Everything will go back to normal."

I feel even worse. My stomach hurts more than ever, because it's my fault we're here in the first place. I need to say something, but I'm scared of how disappointed they'll be.

After dinner, I go to my new temporary room and start writing in the red notebook Mama gave me. I decide I need a diary. I have to express how I feel before I burst.

Downstairs the phone rings, and I hear Baba's voice.

He sounds anxious. Tucking my notebook under my arm, I sneak to the top of the steps and listen.

"Yes, of course. I'll ask my wife," I hear him saying. "I just don't understand."

When he hangs up, he tells Mama, "They've worked out how the fire started. It started in the bin!"

"What?" she says. "The bin? How can a fire start in a bin?"

"It's so strange," he says. "I was at work already, so you were the last one there. Were you cooking before you left?"

"Abdallah!" Now Mama's voice rises. "Are you blaming me?"

"I'm just trying to understand how a fire started in my home, in a bin in our kitchen, with my children in the house. That's all!"

I creep back to my beige room and shut my beige door.

My name is Farah Hajjar, I write, *and I definitely do not rock.*

CHAPTER 10

One evening after dinner, the doorbell rings. Thinking it's the Lius, I rush to the front door and yank it open.

There's a man on our front doorstep who looks almost like my father but shorter. He has black, curly hair and thick eyebrows that look like hairy worms across his forehead. He has a big, happy smile on his face and speaks English with an accent, just like Baba.

"Hello! Hello, little girl," he says, bending down to wave a hand in my face. It sounds like "leetle".

"Hello," I say. I keep the door half closed because I don't know who he is. And then I see the Tree.

"I am Mr Najjarian. My son," he says, pointing over his shoulder, "he goes to school with you, yes?"

"Um, yes," I say. By then, Baba is behind me, welcoming him in. They shake hands, and my mother insists he stay for a cup of coffee.

"We want to welcome you to our neighbourhood," Mr Najjarian says. He's actually very sweet, unlike his son. "Bryan says you will stay only a little time here?"

Baba explains that our house burned down. I hurry to the kitchen to help Mama, because if I stay and listen, my stomach will hurt for the rest of the night. As she boils water for coffee, I put three tiny cups and saucers in a tray. (Arabic coffee is so strong that if you drank it in a big mug, Mama says you wouldn't sleep for a week.)

"Thank God those were not ruined in the fire," Mama says. "That's my good set that I got as a wedding gift." She shakes her head. "I'm trying to look at the positive side of all this."

Aaaaaand . . . hello, stomach ache.

I serve Mr Najjarian first, because he's the guest. He gets excited about the coffee. "This is how we drink coffee in my country," he says.

"You're Armenian, yes?" Baba asks. "I could tell from your last name."

"Yes!" And you can tell Mr Najjarian is happy because nobody ever knows where he's from. They start talking about how our Palestinian and Armenian cultures have a lot in common.

The Tree sits on the floor because there are no more seats left. Samir and I sit on the floor too.

"Hey," says the Tree. Samir just stares at him, not saying a word.

"Your face," I tell the Tree.

"What?" His giant mass of hair swivels towards me.

"He can't see your face. It bothers him," I say.

"Oh." The Tree pulls a rubber band out of his pocket. In one smooth move, he pulls his hair back into a green bun at the top of his head. Suddenly I can actually see his whole face. He has big, brown eyes and a tiny brown birthmark on his cheek.

"How's that, dude?" he asks Samir.

It's like someone turned on a light switch. "Wanna see my stickah?" Samir asks. He shows the Tree an emoji sticker on his t-shirt. "It's from my teachah."

"Did you listen to her and work well?" the Tree asks.

"Yeah!" Samir points his thumb in towards his chest. "I listened weel good."

"Cool." The Tree holds up his hand. "High five."

"What?" Samir sits up on his knees. "A what?"

"Here." He pulls Samir's hand and spreads out his fingers, then smacks them with his own palm. "That's like, 'Awesome!'"

"High five!" Samir squeals, excited and demands that I give him a high five. Then he heads over to the adults. "Mama, high five!"

"He's cute," says the Tree.

"Yeah," I say. I'm glad he was being good to Samir.

My little brother is actually very clever, but sometimes older kids and grown-ups talk to him like he's not. I'm relieved that the Tree is not like that.

We both stare at the beige carpet. I wish the adults would finish their conversation. But now they're talking about how the fruits and vegetables taste so much better "back home". We'll be here for a while.

"Did you hear anything about the clubs we have to join?" I ask the Tree.

"The fair is tomorrow." He cracks his knuckles. "I'm signing up for robotics and engineering."

"Cool."

"You?" he asks.

"No idea. I wonder if they have anything about creative writing," I say. "Like a club where we can write stories and poems and stuff."

He gives me a funny look. "Why?"

"What do you mean? Don't you *read*?" I ask.

"Yeah, computer programming manuals and science magazines. Einstein's not an art school, you know."

"Why can't someone like more than one thing – maths and science *and* creative writing?"

He shakes his head and ignores the question like it's not worth discussing.

Now I'm angry. "I'm going to ask if they have a club like that," I say.

"If they don't?" the Tree asks.

"Then . . . I'm going to start one." I don't know how to tell him that I'm writing stories almost every day, and that it's the only thing that makes me feel better.

"Yeah, whatever. You'll be the only member." He stands up and tells his father he needs to go home to start his homework. "Thank you, Mr and Mrs Hajjar," he says to my parents politely.

"Oh, children," Mama says, smiling. "Mr Najjarian and I have discussed lift sharing. You'll be going to school together a couple of days a week – starting tomorrow!"

Holy hummus.

CHAPTER 11

The next day, Mr Najjarian drives us both to school in a car that's even older than ours. Its fender is rusty and the tyres are missing their rims.

The Tree slouches in the back seat, not talking. He doesn't even say "good morning" to me, but his father is very perky and upbeat. He sings along to Armenian music on old, yellowed cassette tapes all the way.

"You must be a morning person," I tell him.

"Oh no," he says, laughing. "I just finished working. I will go home now and go to bed for six hours."

"Where do you work?" I ask, and I feel the Tree cringe.

"I am a rubbish collector, so I work every night from midnight until seven a.m.," Mr Najjarian says. "Come home, shower, read the paper, have breakfast. After Bryan goes to school, I sleep."

"Oh, wow," I say.

"Wow, what?" the Tree says in a snappy voice.

"Wow, like your dad is on the opposite schedule to the rest of us," I explain.

"So?"

"So nothing," I answer. "Who's that?" I ask his father, pointing to a yellowed photograph taped to the dashboard. The woman in the photo is really pretty. She has a wide smile.

"That lovely lady," says Mr. Najjarian, "is Mrs Najjarian, Bryan's mother." He kisses his fingertips and presses them to the photo. "The love of my life."

I understand enough to know that she is no longer alive. "Oh," I say. "She is beautiful."

"Thank you!" he answers and continues singing until we get to Einstein.

Bryan gets out of the car and closes the door without waiting for me to get out. I push it open again and climb out, while Mr Najjarian says, "I'm so glad Bryan made a nice friend."

He drives away, still singing his songs.

. . .

The Club Fair is being held today, Mr Beaker tells us. He mentions some of the clubs while bouncing a tennis ball against the wall.

"Robotics." *Smack.*

"Chemistry." *Thwap!*

"Astrophysics." *Bam!*

"I'm going to ask today about any creative writing clubs," I tell Allie, whispering so that the Tree, who sits right in front of me, doesn't hear.

"Cool," she says. "I'll join." And I remember once again how I have such a wonderful Official Best Friend.

The Club Fair takes place in the gym, which is also the canteen, after lunch. The tables get pushed up against the walls, and all the clubs put up posters and flyers about what they do. As everyone walks around, Ms Maxim tells us over the microphone that our task is to sign up for at least two clubs by the end of the period.

Allie and I find a geology club, which meets on Thursdays after school. We both sign up for that immediately. The two older kids who run it seem interested in how my last name means "rocks" in Arabic. They tell us that later in the year, they hold a big geology festival called The Rock Stars. Cool!

Allie also signs up for engineering. While she writes her name on the form, I notice the name "Bryan Najjarian" is already on the list.

There aren't any writing clubs, so I walk up to Ms Maxim, who is by the stage talking to Mr Beaker. She wears a beaded necklace that looks like a metal chain with about a hundred turquoise rocks hanging from it in layers. It must weigh a tonne. I wonder how she can even stand up straight!

"Yes?" she asks me.

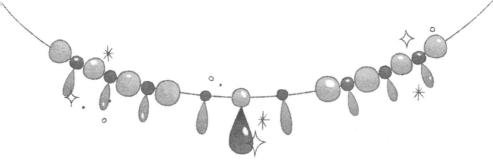

I tear my eyes away from her incredible necklace.

"Farah Rocks," says Mr Beaker. "Find any clubs?"

"Yes," I tell them, "the geology club. But I actually was wondering if I can start a new club?"

"A new club?" asks Ms Maxim, peering down at me like I'm an insect.

I have a bad feeling, and I'm about to tell her, "Never mind!" But then I see Bryan near the robotics table. He smirks at me, shaking his big green head.

Determined, I straighten my shoulders. "Yes, I wanted to join a creative writing club – to write poetry and short stories, maybe even graphic novels. I don't see one here, so I'd like to start one."

"It's a lot of work, Farah," says Mr Beaker. "Maybe it's something you can tackle next year. New students should focus on adjusting to the schoolwork here."

"I want to try," I insist.

He raises his eyebrows and laughs. "Well, then, I like your attitude."

I look at Ms Maxim, who clears her throat, like she's about to make an important statement. "We have guidelines for establishing a new club at the Einstein Academy. New clubs must have a proposal submitted to the Vice Principal for Academic Affairs –" she pauses, then says, "that would be *me* –" and then she continues, "before the stated deadline. It must list the name of the club, its mission–"

"No problem, because–" I say.

"And," she says, raising her hand, "a petition of no fewer than forty student names indicating a genuine interest in the formation of said club."

She stops talking. I wait an extra second, then ask, "Is . . . is that all?"

"I believe so."

"Great. What is the stated deadline?"

She leans towards me. "You have until the tenth of September. One week."

CHAPTER 12

Sitting in church that Sunday, I ignore Father Alexander's sermon and stare at the huge, stained glass window behind the altar. I hate that window.

When Samir was born, three months ahead of his due date, Mama and Baba made a promise to God that they would buy this window for the St Jude Orthodox Church. In return, God had to protect Samir and help him get better.

I guess God thought that was a pretty good deal, because Samir came home a few weeks later. And even when my parents found out how much that window would cost, they stuck to their promise. Being true to your word is a good policy, especially when you're promising something to God.

During the sermon, I try instead to think of ways that I can get thirty-eight other students (besides Allie and me) excited about my idea of a writing club.

"Lord, have mercy!" Father Alexander chants. Everyone repeats after him, except me. I am busy making a mental list of who would be willing to sign up for an extra club. Allie (*duh*), Winston Suarez (*maybe*), June Jordan (*yes, because she's named after a poet*), Rajesh (*yes – he seems artistic*).

Thirty-five to go. It's only my first week at Einstein. I don't even know thirty-five people yet.

When mass ends, Father Alexander makes some announcements. There will be an autumn festival for the kids this year, and we can wear our Halloween costumes. Mrs Saleeba is not feeling well, so everyone can sign a get-well card for her. Mrs Khoury is holding a fundraising lunch at her house in two weeks, and Lana is selling raffle tickets.

I sigh. Lana is my nemesis, like Arachne is to Athena in Greek mythology.

"Also," says Father Alexander, "as we said last week, we are holding an appeal for the Hajjar family, whose home suffered a fire recently." He smiles kindly at us, but I want to crawl under the pew and disappear. "There is a box in the lobby to donate clothes for Farah and Samir. We hope they will be able to move back into their home soon. When, Abdallah?"

"In two to three months, inshallah," says Baba. "Thank you, Father."

"I pray that the repairs move quickly," says Father.

"Amen!" chirps Samir, and everyone laughs.

I don't want to go to coffee hour. Most people mean well, but I get tired of hearing, "Oh, you poor, poor, poor thing!" Mama keeps telling me to eat something but my stomach is hurting too much. I just stare at the church members who pat our shoulders, trying to be sweet.

Mrs Hassan, who is about 150 years old, says in a loud voice, "Oh, I found some size ten trousers in my daughter's wardrobe. Brand new! They're bright orange and blue, and my daughter never wore them. I bet they'll be perfect for Farah!"

Holy hummus.

I smile at Mrs Hassan but give my mother an "I'm-never-ever-ever-ever-wearing-those" look.

As my mother stammers her way out of that one, I lead Samir out to the church's playground. It's really a swing set Father Alexander built by hand. Last year, he added some plastic slides and climbing equipment. It's mostly for the toddlers, but at least it gets me out of the church and gives me time alone.

Besides, I'm still trying to think about how I will get people to sign up for the writing club. Maybe Ms Toste will let me interrupt her push-ups in class and make an announcement. Or maybe, just maybe, I can make an announcement in front of the school somehow, to get a lot of attention at once.

As the idea forms in my head, I suddenly see trouble coming my way.

Lana Khoury, who wouldn't normally be caught dead in the toddler playground, struts over with two of her cousins. Their names are Catie and Paula, but because they always dress exactly like Lana, I call them Copy and Paste. Today they're all wearing woolly boots, glittery leggings and flowery blouses. Their hair is flat and straight and flowy. Mine is so wild and curly that Mama gave up on it this morning and put it in a big bun the size of a doughnut on top of my head. I look down at my ugly dress. It's the one I wear every third Sunday. It just came back from the dry cleaners last night, so it's not smoky any more, but it still has a stupid bow in the back.

Suddenly I hate my life.

"Sorry to hear about your house, Farah," says Lana in a way that doesn't sound very sorry. She's always hated me, but it's got worse since the summer when she was caught sabotaging my tutoring business.

"Thanks," I say, helping Samir climb up the plastic slide.

"It was a tiny house. Probably didn't need more than five minutes to burn," she says to Copy and Paste, in a voice that's loud enough for me to know she wanted me to hear it.

"I wish that dress had got burned," mutters Paste.

"Don't worry, Farah," Lana adds, and I get ready for a blow. "You'll be out of that crummy neighbourhood soon enough. My mum said three months. You'll be back in your house in time for Halloween."

I roll my eyes and blurt out, "Actually, we'll be back a little before Christmas. It's September now, so three months is ninety days. Thirty days in a month, times three. That would put us in December, not October."

I pause while she absorbs my words. Then I add, "I'm pretty good at maths. It's why I got into Einstein."

Her jaw drops open. As if on command, Copy's and Paste's jaws do the same.

I suddenly feel bad. It's not like me to be so harsh,

even with Lana. I don't know how to take it back so I grab Samir's hand and walk away quickly.

"You're a real piece of work, Farah Hajjar!" Lana calls after me. "You know what?" she adds, her face all pink with anger. "I donated some old clothes for you. At least for once in your life, you'll look nice."

I wish I had an answer for that.

Later, as we're leaving church, Mama puts a whole box of clothes, toys and books in the boot. "Wow, people are very generous." She says it so kindly. For a second, I'm furious with her. Doesn't she know that people are making fun of us?

"Yes, they were all bery nice to us," Baba agrees.

I groan. Baba gives me a funny look, so I just get in the car silently.

At home, Mama gives me a pile of clothes that people have donated. One of the shirts is long-sleeved and black, and says *bebe* in rhinestones across the front. There is another piece of clothing, a long, flowy black dress with a zigzag hem that has a Chanel label.

I know they are from Lana, because I've seen her wear them both. I take the bag and jam it deep in my beige wardrobe and shut the beige door.

CHAPTER 13

In maths class, Mr Beaker returns a test that we took the day before. We're having a test every week, he explained, because we need to finish this topic and start a new one.

He puts the paper face-down on my desk, and I turn it over.

Holy hummus. My result is seventy-five.

Allie gasps and shows me hers: seventy-eight.

Everyone looks horrified, so Mr Beaker says, "You may have got good grades easily in your other schools. But at Einstein, here's the hard truth: Everyone here is good at maths. Not just you."

"Maybe we shouldn't start a new club," Allie says to me later at our lockers. "We might need more time to study than we're used to."

Maybe she's right, I think. And yet, writing stories and reading books . . . they make me feel better about everything. I want to make time for this. I *need* to make time for it.

"No," I tell Allie firmly. "We've got to do this. Maths and science are important, but stories matter too!"

. . .

By lunchtime on Monday, I have signatures from eleven students: me, Allie and nine other people. In English class, I ask Ms Toste if I can make an announcement. "Sure," she says and starts doing squats while I talk. She exhales on the way down and inhales on the way up.

"Everyone," I say to the class, but they all stare at Ms Toste. "Hey, guys!" I call loudly. All eyes focus on me. "We're starting a new club, but we need forty signatures to get it approved." Behind me, I hear Ms Toste counting under her breath as she reaches ten squats.

"It's a writing club," I continue, "and we'll do things like write stories, plays, poems, maybe comics. It'll be a lot of fun. Anyone interested in signing up?"

I hold up the sheet. The room is as quiet as a cemetery.

"We might even start our own magazine," adds Allie helpfully.

"Sounds fun, Farah," says Amanda. "But we already have so much schoolwork, you know? Who has time?"

I lower the paper, and my heart feels like a popped balloon.

In the back of the room, Bryan smirks.

Suddenly, Enrique stands up and walks towards me. "Hey, I'll sign up, Farah Rocks. Sounds cool." He takes the paper from me, puts it down on Ms Toste's desk, and signs it.

Suddenly four girls agree to sign up. Then two

guys and then three more girls. I don't know if they're signing up because of Enrique, who is already one of Einstein's popular people, or because of the club itself.

But I don't care. Within five minutes, I have twenty-one names. Almost the whole class.

Two days to go.

. . .

At dinner, Mama makes warak dawali, or stuffed grape leaves. I like to pour lemon juice on them and pop them into my mouth like chicken nuggets.

"Yummy!" says Samir.

"Bery good!" Baba adds, taking a bite and giving Mama a thumbs-up.

As we eat, she asks me why I haven't worn any of my new clothes.

"You mean my old new clothes that people donated?" I ask, and I hate how sarcastic I sound. I don't mean it that way.

"Farah," she says in her library-quiet voice. "Samir

is wearing a sweater today that Mrs Ibrahim gave him. Nothing wrong with that."

"Well, Mrs Khoury and Lana donated most of mine, and I don't want them," I say.

"Ahh, the famous Mrs Khoury," Baba says with a laugh.

"What's so funny?" Mama asks him.

"Oh, nothing," he answers. Then he stands up on his tiptoes and walks across the room in a dainty way. "Oh, habibti, I might be late for my manicure. Let me check the time." He exaggerates the way he stretches out his wrist to check an imaginary watch. "Oh, yes, it's a new watch. Cartier, don't you know?"

I start laughing. Mama shakes her head, but she's grinning.

"How much?" he goes on. "For this little thing? Oh, only thirty thousand dollars!"

Mama laughs so hard that she starts coughing.

"Come back to the table, Mrs Khoury," I tell Baba. "Have some more dawali."

"Oh, this dawali is the best!" Baba exclaims, pre-tending to flick his imaginary long hair. "It was made by my bersonal chef."

"Your personal chef says hurry up and eat instead of making fun of people," Mama says.

He shrugs and gets back to his food. "That is the silliest woman I eber met," he says.

Later, we all help clean up. As Baba loads the dishwasher, he bangs a plate against the worktop and it shatters. Baba is famous for breaking dishes in our house. We all gasp and stare at the white shards on the floor.

And then we burst out laughing. The kind of laughing that's half crying. And at that moment, I know that I'd rather be here in our beige underworld house on L Street than in Lana Khoury's big, fancy mansion.

Or anywhere else on Earth.

CHAPTER 14

I spend the rest of the evening practising maths, again and again until I understand what I did wrong in the test. We don't have Wi-Fi in this house, so Baba drives me to Allie's house to watch some videos that Mr Beaker recommended. Watching someone work out the problems and talking through it helps me a lot.

Allie and I decide to do a practice test. We set her clock timer for thirty minutes and start. When the timer beeps, we check our answers in the back of the book. My score goes up to an 88 and hers to an 89.

"We should practise like this two or three nights a week," Allie says. "That's the only way."

"And weekends," I tell her. It's strange that we finally have to work hard to get good results.

Later, we brainstorm ideas for the creative writing club. We need nineteen more signatures by Friday.

"Maybe Ms Maxim will let us make a morning announcement," Allie says.

"What would we say?" I wonder out loud, putting my maths books in my backpack. Jammed in the back is my Greek mythology book. I take it out and flip through it. I see a picture of Medusa, and I show it to Allie.

"Gross," she says.

"She was so ugly that looking at her would turn people to stone," I say.

"Some people are that ugly on the inside," she adds.

Of course, I think about Lana Khoury.

I tell Allie what Lana said. "I don't even want to go to church this weekend because I hate seeing her."

"You can wear mine," she says, opening her wardrobe. She holds up a blue one with small flowers along the skirt. "This one is great. You have blue shoes?"

"No," I say, standing up and taking the beautiful dress. "I only have my black ones and my trainers."

"We're still the same size." She digs through her cupboard and finds a pair of flat, blue shoes with a white buckle. "There you go. Problem solved."

"I'll look after them carefully!" I promise and hug her so hard that I almost knock her down.

"Farah Rocks!" she shrieks, giggling. From downstairs, Mr Liu calls, "You girls okay?"

"Yes!" we shout in unison.

Still laughing, I put the mythology book in my backpack, then thoughtfully, I take it out again. I flip open to the chapter on Zeus. In the illustration, he is gripping a thunderbolt in his hand, ready to rocket it down to Earth.

"Holy hummus," I say out loud. I have an idea.

．•．

The next morning, we ask Ms Maxim if we can make an announcement to the school.

"About?" she asks.

"About our new club," I say.

"Still pursuing that, are you?" She shrugs. "I can give you two minutes."

"Thank you!"

"Don't forget that your application is due tomorrow," she says. "I won't accept it after that."

"Yes, of course." I try to sound confident, but I'm not really.

A group of four older kids recite a reading, and then another kid reads the lunch menu for the day. Then Ms Maxim says into the microphone, "And now, we have a short announcement by two students, Farah Hajjar and Allie Liu."

She hands me the microphone. I nod to Allie, who uses her mum's mobile phone to play a tune.

Here is what the students at the Einstein Academy hear: a huge *boom* of thunder, followed by several shorter bursts. Ms Maxim looks annoyed. The secretary, who is startled, stops clicking on her mouse and stares. Some kids in the year above, who were on their way back to class, freeze and gape at us.

I take the microphone. "That sound is scary, yeah? It startles us, even though we know what it is – thunder. We know what causes it too. But what did humans do before science explained everything?"

I take a deep breath. Allie gives me a thumbs-up, and I go on. "They made up stories. The Greeks invented Zeus, the chief god on Mount Olympus. They believed he would throw down bolts of lightning whenever silly humans angered him."

Allie takes the microphone. "We all use stories to explain what we don't know and what we worry about. We also use stories just to have fun. I'm Allie Liu, and this is Farah Hajjar. We're forming a new club at Einstein – a creative writing club. We'll write stories and poems and plays, and maybe even start our own magazine."

My turn: "See one of us today at lunch or break time, but make sure you don't wait! We need you to join today, because our application is due in the morning."

We hand the microphone back to Ms Maxim, whose face doesn't really have an expression. But on our way out, a couple of girls ask us if they can join the club. Allie hands them the petition, and they add their names to the list.

"We'll tell our friends too," says one of the girls.

Another girl adds, "Cool idea. We've never had anything like this at Einstein."

We are thunderstruck.

At lunch that day, a few more people sign up for our club.

"What'cha got there?" asks Mrs Salvatore. Today, her Shakespeare badge says, *To thine own self be true.*

"We're starting a creative writing club," Allie tells her with a smile.

"Brava!" she says, smiling. "We need something like that round here."

At the end of the day, we have thirty-nine signatures. We are one away from the goal.

CHAPTER 15

After school, Samir and I look for rocks. We find some, and I run inside and fill a plastic bowl with water and washing-up liquid. This is one of our favourite things to do – clean and polish rocks. We sit on the step and carefully wash each one. Samir is working hard on a peach-coloured one, which I think may be orthoclase. We never had any of those near our old house.

As I polish, I try to think of a way to talk to my parents. I have to tell them about the fire. The longer I keep it a secret, the more it grows. It's like a rock that builds layers and layers of sediment. The more dense it grows, the harder it is to break.

I pretend not to notice when Bryan comes out of his house and starts kicking a football into the net.

A group of three boys rides by on their bikes, laughing and hooting at each other. I don't recognize them. One of them, a boy with shaved hair, is the leader of the group.

"They not wearing helmets, Faw-wah," says Samir softly.

"How silly of them," I answer.

I watch them drop their bikes on the quad, not far from where Bryan is kicking his ball. One of the boys takes cans of drink out of a plastic bag hanging over his handlebars, and he hands one to each of his friends. They lean on their bikes, drinking and sharing a bag of crisps while watching Bryan. They stare at him strangely, and not just because he has green hair. It's like they're daring him to speak.

He ignores them and continues his kicks, even though they're just about a metre away from him.

The kid with the shaved hair drains his can in one

gulp and casually throw it onto the grass. The other two laugh and follow his lead, and then they even throw their crisp packets on the ground too.

"Hey!" Bryan breaks the silence. "Don't litter here, Ronnie!"

"Why not?" the kid asks. "Because it's a trashy neighbourhood."

Holy hummus.

His words are so ugly I want to scream.

"Anyway, you can pick it up, right? Start practising to be a rubbish collector like your dad." He kicks Bryan's ball, and it lands in a pile of wet, muddy leaves.

All three burst out laughing and take off on their bikes, hopping over the kerb that borders the quad and back onto the pavement. As we all watch, they cycle past K Street, then J Street, and finally out of the area.

Bryan kicks the ball one last time into the net and glances up at us. Samir and I just look back at him silently, unsure of what to do. Maybe Bryan and I have more in common than I thought. He's had to deal with people who remind me of Lana.

He stomps back to his house, slamming the front door behind him.

Samir and I walk over to the quad, and I quickly pick up the cans and crisp packets and put them in the recycling and rubbish bins. Samir takes Bryan's football and walks back to our steps. He sits and rubs it with his cloth and the soapy water until it's shiny.

Some people don't think my brother is very clever, but he is. And he's very kind too. This is what I think as I watch him walk over and leave the shiny-as-new ball on Bryan Najjarian's front doorstep.

. . .

When Baba gets home, he suggests we go to the labyrinth, one of my favourite places in Harbourtown. It's a small rock garden with a twisted, spiral walkway that was built last year behind the library.

Samir wants to walk with me, so I hold his hand as we set out on the path. You have to take it easy so you don't get dizzy, because you are walking in smaller and smaller circles until you get to the middle. As I walk, I think about all the wild things that have happened in just the past two weeks:

- I'm working hard for the first time to get good results.
- I'm trying to start a club that not many people think belongs at Einstein.
- I probably won't be able to start it because I still need a signature.
- I've made an enemy of sorts.
- I don't actually want Bryan to be my enemy.
- Oh, and I set my family's house on fire.

In the labyrinth's centre is a stone bench, where Samir and I sit for a while, watching as Mama and Baba finish their walk. In the quiet, I can't avoid thinking about the fire any longer.

There is a horrible feeling in my stomach. It's been there since I saw Mr Liu drench that match in water. I can tell my parents are stressed out because they're waiting for the insurance money to arrive. We need it to buy new clothes and furniture and other things.

They're frustrated, even though they try not to show it. Baba has to leave extra early for work, because this house is further away. And I can hear Mama sighing in the kitchen when she doesn't have enough room to put away her pans.

But they pretend that it's all okay. Because they're trying to make Samir and me feel better.

"Let's go?" Baba asks when he and Mama reach us.

"You slowcoaches!" Samir says, giggling.

Baba grabs him and tickles him, saying, "You're calling *me* a slowcoach? I'll show you!" and then he gives him a ride to the car on his shoulders.

While Baba drives, Mama says, "Farah, I wish you could start wearing some of the clothes they gave us at church. Lana's clothes would fit you. I'm doing a lot of laundry because you keep wearing the same things over and over again."

"No," I say flatly, wishing she would not bring this up, when the day had ended so nicely. I'm sorry she has to do more laundry, but I just can't wear Lana's clothes.

"Please, Farah. You're being unreasonable."

"Mama, please," I answer irritably. "I'm not wearing anything from Lana or any of her stupid cousins."

"Farah, you're being silly," she says sternly.

"I'm NOT wearing Lana's clothes!" I actually shout.

Mama gasps at my tone. Baba pulls over into the car park of the Harbourtown supermarket. He parks the car and sits for a minute. We're all quiet.

I feel like the most awful person in the world. I wish they would just leave me here in the car park and take off.

Then Baba speaks. "In the Hajjar family, we do not scream at each other. In this family, we do not let a bad time make us bad beoble." Then he looks at me in the mirror. "I will keeb saying it to you: we are lucky to be safe. Nothing else matters."

I nod, ashamed of myself. I feel horrible, but I don't know how to say it. We drive home silently.

When we pull up in front of our house on L Street,

we see a small, white paper tucked between the door and the doorframe.

Farah and Samir,

You both rock. Thanks.

- Bryan

CHAPTER 16

The next morning, Mr Najjarian sings "Good Morning" all the way to school. Bryan sits in the back seat again. He doesn't look at me, but his hair is in a bun again, showing his face.

"We got your note," I tell him.

"Good," he says.

That's it. He doesn't mention the kids on the bikes, and I don't ask any questions.

As his father pulls up in the drop-off line, Bryan suddenly asks, "How's your petition going?"

Surprised, I tell him we are one signature short. "Why?" I ask.

He holds up a pen. "Give me the paper."

Holy hummus. He signs his name on line number forty.

"Thanks, Bryan!" I say, my eyes wide.

I realize that I haven't thought of him as Tree for a while now. I don't even remember when I started thinking of him as Bryan. Maybe it was the day I learnt about his mum.

I run to class and ask Mr Beaker if Allie and I can go to the main office.

"Hurry back," he says.

I practically drag Allie out of her seat and into the corridor. As we leave the classroom, I glance back at Bryan, who's grinning.

"What's up?" she asks, out of breath.

"We got it," I whisper-shout in the corridor.

"Got it? You mean . . . you mean . . . ?"

"The fortieth signature," I confirm.

She hops up and down from sheer excitement. "Who?" she demands to know as we rush to the office.

"You'll never guess."

. . .

Ms Maxim didn't jump for joy or anything, but she approved the club and assigned us a room where we could meet once a week after school. We are given a small budget to buy snacks for our meetings and do projects, like printing a school magazine. "They still don't know which of the teachers will be our advisor," I tell Mama when she picks me up after school, "but we have time to find one."

Mama is very quiet, only nodding when I speak.

"You okay, Mama?" I ask her.

"Yes," she says. No "habibti", no "darling".

From the rearview mirror, I watch as a fat tear rolls down her cheek.

"The insurance company finally called me back," she said, "and the pay-out won't come for at least two more weeks. It's just going to be tough for a little longer to pay our bills."

"I'm sorry, Mama."

She sniffs. "We'll be okay."

The rock in my stomach weighs a tonne.

At dinner, Baba is quiet too, but Samir is bubbly as he talks about his school's Halloween plans. "The whole year is having a big pawty!" he exclaims. "With costumes."

He waits for us, looking like a cute elf. "Want to know what my costume is?"

"Yes, Samir," says Mama.

"You do?"

"Yes."

"So?" He waits and stares at her. "Ask me."

She bursts out laughing. "Fine. What are you going to be?"

Samir looks at Baba. "Ask me, Baba."

Baba grins as he swallows his forkful of rice. "What are you going to be for Halloween, my handsome son?"

Samir looks at me next. "Faw-wah?"

I give in and ask.

"OKAY . . . TOMMY TURTLE!" Samir yells.

"Cool idea!" I tell him. But I notice Mama and Baba glance worriedly at each other.

I know what they are thinking. A real costume will cost a lot of money.

"Samir, let's *make* your Tommy Turtle costume! We'll do it together," I suggest in an excited voice. "We can start after dinner!"

"*Make* it? But my fwiends said you have to *buy* it from the shop."

"Yes, everyone will buy it," I say, rolling my eyes. "But *yours* will be extra special because we'll make it ourselves. So let's finish eating and get started!"

"Kapow!" he exclaims.

Later we sit in the tiny living room, sketching out how his costume will look. Mama puts a plate of sliced apples in front of us and drops a kiss on my forehead.

CHAPTER 17

A week later, in class, Allie and I get a letter from Ms Maxim, reminding us to choose an advisor for the creative writing club.

Allie suggests Ms Toste, but I say, "For an English teacher, she doesn't really seem into writing." But Allie wants to ask anyway, so we find her during lunch.

In her classroom, she's sitting at her chair, doing bicep curls with the small dumbbells that she keeps under her desk. "Sorry, girls," she says after explaining she's too busy advising the fitness club.

We head to the canteen, which is

decorated in orange and black streamers for Halloween. "What should we be this year?" Allie asks me as we sit at a table near the window. "A maths equation?"

Allie and I usually have coordinated costumes. In third grade, we were a peanut butter and jam sandwich. She wore a large cardboard bread slice with purple pom-poms all over it. I wore the same bread slice covered with brown felt. In fourth grade, she was two hydrogen atoms (she wore two Hs on her shirt), I was a large O that we cut out of a box, and we carried water bottles around. Nobody in our year even understood.

"I need something simple," I tell Allie. I tell her how I'm helping Samir make a Tommy Turtle costume because my parents don't have the insurance money yet. "Like a witch or a pumpkin."

"Or a ghost?"

"That would be good," I say. I'd need only a white sheet and a marker pen.

Mrs Salvatore, the dinner lady with the velvet hat, walks past us and waves. The badge on her hat today says, *By the pricking of my thumbs, something wicked this way comes.*

"More Shakespeare?" I ask her.

"Yep!" she says, patting her hat. "*Macbeth.* There's a scene where the witches stir up a brew." She grins. "I studied drama at university and love theatre," she explains.

"That's brilliant, Mrs Salvatore," Allie says.

I realize she is staring at the nice dinner lady with the same expression I'm wearing: total delight.

When she walks away, Allie says to me, "Are you thinking what I'm thinking?"

I nod. "Let's get to the main office."

Ms Maxim doesn't seem thrilled. "An advisor should be a faculty member," she says.

"But Mrs Salvatore studied literature and drama," I argue. "And she *does* work here."

"I have to think about it." She waves us away. "A story club. At the Einstein Academy," we hear her mutter as we close the door behind us.

. . .

That night, while helping Samir make his costume, I think about the witches in *Macbeth*. Witches who cast spells on people. I think witches are powerful, and I'd be one if I could. I wouldn't be wicked, though. I would be a good witch who makes things right again.

As I help Samir colour in a big cardboard circle that will be his shell, I think of all the problems I would fix:

- Make the insurance money arrive quickly.
- Change the past so that the house never burnt down in the first place.
- Stop kids from bullying Bryan about his father's job.
- Help Mrs Salvatore have her dream of being an actress.

"I need scissors. I'll be right back," I tell Samir and head to my room. I notice the bag of clothes from church in my cupboard. An idea hits me. I tear open the bag and pull out the black trousers and shirt from Lana.

Maybe I can be a witch after all, I think, and I grab the scissors.

CHAPTER 18

Ms Maxim reluctantly gives our creative writing club permission to begin meeting before we have an advisor.

Our first meeting, held in the library, opens with an argument.

And Bryan starts it. "We need a good name," he announces.

Everyone agrees and starts shouting out ideas.

"We'll call ourselves the Poetic Justices!"

"The Word Players!"

Meanwhile Allie says, logically, that we should talk about our goals before we choose a name.

"What will we be doing?" asks June.

"We can start by sharing our writing once a week," I suggest. "So every week, everyone swaps a piece of writing with someone else in the group."

"We should publish something," June says. "The robotics club writes a blog. We could write for a month, pick some good pieces and print our own magazine."

Everyone seems to like this idea, and we make plans. Everyone will bring in a poem, story or essay by next week, and we'll share ideas on how to make them better.

"What topics are we going to write about?" asks Enrique.

"Write whatever you care about, whatever is on your mind," suggests June.

"I care about tennis," says Enrique. "Is that okay?"

We all nod. "Yeah, write about that," Allie says.

"Can we write about stress?" asks Rajesh. "Einstein is kind of stressful," he adds, looking around hesitantly.

"Yeah," says one of the older kids. "I feel like I'm under pressure all the time to do well here."

"Me too," says Enrique, shrugging his shoulders.

"You don't feel like you can just enjoy learning," says June. "I didn't even tell my mother I've joined a writing club."

"Why not?" asks Bryan.

"Because she named me *June Jordan*," she answers. "She'll be after me to write a book. Talk about pressure."

"That would be like if my parents had named me Albert Einstein," says Rajesh. "Albert Einstein Gupta," he adds, making us all laugh.

Allie says, "I think we have a theme here after all."

. . .

Allie and I spend the evening at her house, working on maths to get ready for Mr Beaker's test. The problems are long and tricky, and I'm frustrated. I used to be able to look at a problem and just see the numbers arrange themselves in my head, but these are so complicated.

"I need a break," Allie says, throwing her notebook on the floor. "Juice?"

"Yes, please."

While she goes downstairs, I pull out my writing notebook and write:

The rock in my stomach feels worse and worse, and my parents are so stressed out that they had an actual argument last night about Samir's therapy and how expensive it is getting. Every time Mama says she will work overtime, Baba gets upset. I think he feels bad that she is working so much.

I hear Allie coming back upstairs, so I add, *I wish that stupid money would just arrive!* and stick the red notebook in my backpack.

. . .

The money finally comes in a week before Halloween. Baba goes to the bank to sort it out. I see Mama smile in relief.

Mr Najjarian comes over for coffee that evening and he tells my parents that not much trick-or-treating happens on L Street. "Bryan doesn't go anyway," he said. "Maybe now he's too old for trick-or-treating?"

"Nobody is too old for that," Baba claims and invites

him to come to our old neighbourhood.

"I will ask Bryan," he says. "These are the days when I miss my wife the most." He sighs sadly, and Baba pats his shoulder.

I am finishing up my costume at the small table. I imagine growing up without a mother. I'm trying to understand Bryan. He still doesn't talk to me much, but he did sit with Allie and me on the patio at lunch. I also noticed he's been hanging out with Rajesh and Enrique.

Maybe it was hard for him to make friends at his old school, I think. *Especially if a lot of them were like those kids on the bikes.*

Maybe the Einstein Academy is the best thing that's happened to him so far.

. . .

The creative writing club is going really well. The members have exchanged work twice already, and everyone is being very helpful.

"I think this sentence is really good, but the ending

could be more exciting."

"This line doesn't help me paint a picture in my head. Maybe more details?"

"Great story! I like the character's name."

Allie and I are thrilled, even though Ms Maxim still does not seem too excited.

When we reported to her that some of our budget money would be spent on printing a small magazine, she shrugged. "OK."

"We also would like to ask again if Mrs Salvatore can be our advisor," I say.

Ms Maxim straightens the silver brooch on her suit jacket and glares at me. "I'm still considering it."

Allie and I don't ask any more questions.

The Thursday before Halloween, the club finally selects a name: Milky Way. It's Rajesh's idea, because as he says, "We want to write about everything in the galaxy."

"I like it," says Bryan, which makes it feel final.

"Maybe you can design a logo for us," I tell Rajesh,

and he grins.

At the end of the meeting, we exchange work with everyone. It is my turn to exchange something with Bryan, and he hands me a single sheet of paper.

"What's this?" I ask.

"A poem."

"A poem?"

"Yes, it's a form of writing done in lines, instead of paragraphs," he jokes. "Sometimes it rhymes, and sometimes it doesn't."

"I know what a poem is," I say. "I just didn't know you write poetry."

Allie calls for me. "Quick question, Farah!"

"Coming!" I turn back to Bryan. "My club notebook is on my chair. Just grab it."

"No problem," he says. "I can't wait to see what Farah Rocks writes about."

. . .

That night, before I start my homework, I take out

Bryan's poem and read it.

I am stunned by how deeply Bryan must miss his

A Wish

I wish to know
If a memory is real or if I have only
Imagined it.

It's my mother, holding me up
As I try to cross the monkey bars.
My own weight pulls me down, and my hands lose their grip
Over and over
But she keeps me up so I do not fall.
Not once do I fall.
I cross to the other side.
She claps for me and cheers.
And I feel amazing.

Is it a dream, or
Did she really carry me
And make me
A champion?

mother. Somehow, reading this poem has made Bryan seem more real to me, not just a sarcastic person who cares only about science and numbers.

Suddenly I know for sure – more sure than I have felt in a long time – that the creative writing club has been worth it.

I unzip my backpack to look for my red notebook, so I can describe this new revelation about Bryan. But it's not there. I hurry downstairs and ask Mama for her car keys. Maybe it fell out in the car on the way home.

Nothing.

I start to panic. I call Allie, but she doesn't have it. "Didn't you have it out at the Milky Way meeting?" she asks. "Wasn't it on your chair?"

Outside my window, I hear a thud. I part the beige curtains and look down on the quad. It's Bryan, kicking his football into the net, practising despite the icy wind.

The rock in my stomach grows so big that now it's

filling up my heart too.

I think about what I wrote in that notebook.

I threw the candle and matchstick into the bin, and that is what caused the fire. It's all my fault. And nobody knows.

Now, someone does.

CHAPTER 19

Halloween is on a Sunday. That morning, we wear our costumes to church. Father Alexander planned some games for the kids during the coffee hour.

I come down the steps to show my parents my costume. "Farah!" Baba exclaims. "Bery cool!"

Mama also seems amazed. I've lined the black pants with purple sequins, and I've shredded the edges of the long blouse to make it look like a tattered dress. My pointed hat is made with black cardboard, trimmed in purple.

"And now, introducing . . . ," I say in my most dramatic voice, pointing to the steps, "Tommy Turtle!"

Samir runs downstairs in his costume, jumps off the bottom step, and yells, "Kapow!"

Mama and Baba clap excitedly. He really does look great. His shell is made of cardboard, strapped around his waist with Baba's brown belt. He's wearing his green sweatpants, a green T-shirt, and a yellow bandana around his eyes for the face mask.

Samir high-fives my parents, because that's his favourite thing to do now. "Kapow!" he yells every time.

"Kabow!" Baba shouts back.

As we get into the car for church, I see Bryan practising his kicks again on the quad. While Mama is inside getting her purse, I hurry over.

"Whoa! Don't put a curse on me!" he sniggers.

"Do you have my red notebook?" I demand.

"Yep."

"Oh."

And we both stare at each other through the net.

"You should tell your parents what you did."

"I know," I say. "I will."

He shrugs. "Unless you do, you're technically lying."

"Thanks a lot, genius," I answer. Then more carefully, I ask, "You won't tell your dad or anything?"

"No." He shrugs. "And you won't tell anyone about my poem? I've decided I don't want it shared with the rest of the club."

"Deal."

"Deal."

As I start to walk away, I pause and turn around. "I really loved it. Your poem. It was beautiful."

He looks at me, then down at the ground. "Thanks," he mumbles before smacking the ball again into the net.

. . .

At church, I groan out loud when I see Lana. She's also a witch. Except she is a fancy witch. Her costume obviously came from a shop: short skirt with green and black glitter, matching green and black striped leggings, tall hat and a silver wig.

Behind her are Copy and Paste, and – surprise – they're fancy witches too.

Lana seems taller than usual because she's wearing high-heeled black boots. I look down at my usual trainers, around which I've taped black cardboard. The cardboard on my left shoe is already tearing off.

Lana and her mother exchange a snooty smile as my family sits in our pew. I ignore her and focus on Father Alexander. "It's fun to dress up as someone you're not," he says. He waves at Samir and other kids, who are dressed as superheroes, pumpkins and princesses.

"But remember," he says, pausing to be dramatic, "that no matter who you try to be, people will only ever notice how kindly or how badly you treat them."

Mama slides her hand into mine. She tilts her head towards Mrs Khoury and Lana and shrugs. I laugh to myself because Mama never misses a thing.

If I were a witch, and I could have a house like Mrs Khoury's, I wouldn't take it. I wouldn't trade Mama for all the Mrs Khourys in the world.

CHAPTER 20

On Halloween night, we meet at the Lius' for trick-or-treating. Bryan and his father have said they will join us. While we wait for them, we watch Mr Liu carve a pumpkin. *It's like a piece of art,* I think, as I see him create a picture of a black cat's shadow against the full moon.

"Now, for the final touch!" he says. He puts a small tea-light candle inside the hollowed-out pumpkin. It looks like a full moon shining behind the black cat.

"Very imbressive," Baba tells Mr Liu. Mama and Mrs Liu come in to see, and Allie reenters the kitchen, also dressed as a witch. We all stare in awe at the gorgeous pumpkin.

"Hey, Faw-wah!" Samir giggles. "Wemember when you lit the candle at home and we sang happy birthday? Do that voice again, Faw-wah!"

Mrs Liu smiles in confusion, and asks, "What voice? Farah, you do a voice?"

Mama and Baba are staring at me in shock.

"What voice, Farah?" Mrs. Liu asks again.

"*What candle?*" Mama asks in her creepily quiet voice.

Holy hummus. "I . . . I . . ." I stutter, but just then Samir chimes in.

"Wemember my birthday? When you went out, Faw-wah lit a candle on my cake and she sang to me. And then we covered the icing back up so Mama wouldn't see it."

Everyone freezes.

He gasps, clapping his hands to his cheeks. "Oh no! It was a secwet! Sorry, Faw-wah."

"It's okay," I say weakly.

"What happened, Farah?" Baba asks me in Arabic, but the Lius seem to understand him anyway.

The words tumble out of me. "I lit a candle to sing 'Happy Birthday', and . . . and I threw the candle out in the bin afterwards. I realized later that I probably should have run some water over it –"

"Because it can still smoulder," Mr Liu said, shaking his head. "The candle could have set any paper products in the bin on fire."

Baba is quiet. Mama is quiet. The Lius are quiet.

"I'm so sorry," I say in a rush. Then I start to cry. "I've been keeping it inside all this time."

Mrs Liu waves to her husband and Allie. They slip out of the room, leaving us alone.

"Two months," Mama says. "You've been keeping this from us for *two whole months*."

"That's lying," Baba says flatly. He leaves the room. After giving me a stern look, Mama follows him out. My heart feels like it's shredded more than my shirt is.

A few minutes later, the doorbell rings. I see Allie in the foyer, answering it. It's Mr Najjarian.

"Where's Bryan?" Allie asks.

"On the pavement," Mr Najjarian says after shaking hands with the Lius. The rest of us huddle in the hallway to see him. "He says he won't fit inside."

"What?" Allie and I both exclaim. Everyone steps outside to see why not.

There's nothing there except a metal rubbish bin.

 When Samir walks up to it, the lid pops off and Bryan's head sticks out. "Boo!" he says.

"Kapow!" Samir yells back.

Everyone laughs in delight. Bryan has cut out holes for his arms, and the bottom of the bin has also been cut out to make room for his legs. He's wearing a cotton hat, and the metal lid is attached to it.

"I just curl up inside," he explains. "When I hear people coming, I stand up and stick my head out."

"What a fantastic costume!" Mama tells him. "You are a clever boy, Bryan." She catches my eye, then looks away.

I look at Baba, who is sort of smiling, but he also won't look at me.

"Let's start trick-or-treating!" Mr Liu says. Up and down the street, people are coming out of their homes. The area is filling up with monsters, robots, vampires and princesses.

"Yes! Yes!" Samir exclaims, bouncing up and down.

We cover most of the neighbouring streets. My parents don't speak to me, but they laugh and chat with everyone else. I know they don't want to ruin the night for the others. Our bags are getting heavier and heavier as we knock on what seems like hundreds of doors.

At one point, Bryan taps my shoulder. "Look over there," he says, pointing.

Ahead of us, we see three kids on bikes, wearing scary masks with fake blood dripping down bone-white faces. They screech by the huddles of little kids dressed as trains and pumpkins and scream, "Boo!"

One little boy, dressed as a bunny, starts to cry. His father yells at the bikers, "What's wrong with you kids?"

"Here they come," Bryan whispers. He moves to the edge of the pavement. Then he crouches down until he looks like an ordinary rubbish bin.

The bikers ride up to us, slowing down to shout "Boo!" at Allie, Samir and me. They pump their masks to make the fake blood drip down their faces.

"Go away, you bullies!" Allie shouts at them.

"Go away, you bullies!" one of them says, mimicking her and laughing.

But when they get closer to the rubbish bin, one of the boys kicks the edge of it. And that's when Bryan jumps out and screams at the top of his lungs, "Rawwwwwwrrrrrrrrrr!"

"WHOAAAAAAA!" they all scream, almost falling off their bikes.

The trick-or-treaters laugh at them. They straighten their bikes and pedal off as fast as they can.

"Great trick," I tell Bryan later, when we're all finished laughing.

"And a treat," he adds. "For us."

We walk past our house on Hollow Woods Lane. "There it is," Mama says softly. "Almost done."

I haven't been here in three weeks, I realize. I've been so busy with the club and studying for maths class.

Our home looks fantastic. It looks new. The windows shine, and a new front door has been installed. It's blue, with a small, diamond-shaped glass pane.

"We're almost home," Baba says as well, holding Mama's hand. "It won't be too much longer now."

Samir pops in between them. "I love this house," he says. "But I like living close to Bryan too."

"Bryan can still come and teach you football," Mr Najjarian promises.

"Absolutely," Bryan says and high-fives Samir.

I stand apart from my family, gazing at our house as well. I feel so awful about the last two months: the fire, the lies, the stress and the secrets. If they never spoke to me again, I wouldn't blame them.

But then Baba turns his head and reaches his hand out to me. "Come here, Farah," he says in Arabic.

I take his hand, and he hugs me. "We are okay," he says.

And we are.

. . .

Our club produces the first issue of the *Milky Way Literary Magazine*. We print enough copies for all teachers to share with their classes, and the Einstein librarian requests two copies to display in the library. One day after school, our club buys pizza and drinks, and we spend two hours putting the photocopied papers together and stapling them.

"It's amazing that we've pulled this off," Enrique says to Bryan.

"My first published poem!" June Jordan says excitedly to Allie.

I'm so proud of this club and what we've done so far, in only six weeks.

I hand-deliver a copy of the magazine to Ms Maxim. She's not in the office so I leave it with her secretary, an older woman who skims through it. "Oh, how wonderful!" she says with a smile.

A few days later, I get a note from Ms Maxim in homeroom.

Dear Farah Hajjar and Allie Liu,

I have been impressed with the first issue of the *Milky Way Literary Magazine*. It has been enlightening for us to read about the stresses that Einstein students feel.

Mrs Salvatore has agreed to serve as your advisor, even though it is not part of her regular duties. She is excited, and she explained that she studied theatre, which is something we never realized before.

I think you are not afraid to change things and try new ideas. That is just what we want in our students here at the Einstein Academy.

Write on!
Sincerely,
Ms Maxim

. . .

Mama and Baba read my story in the magazine carefully.

"Farah," Baba says, patting my shoulder.

"Habibti," Mama says, stroking my hair.

I am sorting through all the Halloween sweets I have left. I have separated it into careful piles: chewy sweets, chocolate bars, lollipops and gum.

"Yes?" I reply.

"We love you," they say at the same time.

"Thank you!" I say, my heart feeling full. "I love you too –"

"But," Baba says.

"Don't you ever –" Mama says.

"Eber, eber, eber –" Baba adds.

"Play with matches in the house."

"Or lie to us again."

"A fire is bad," Mama says.

"But losing you would be the worst thing in the

world." Baba looks like he's going to cry. "Not just losing *you*. But losing the honest, truthful Farah we know. That is our Farah, and we don't want her to change in any way."

I nod, feeling really relieved that they have finally told me how they feel.

"You cannot ever hide things from us," Mama says. "We are a family. We always forgive, habibti."

I smile at them widely. "I know."

"Now," Baba says, "we need to discuss a suitable bunishment."

"Oh."

He looks at my piles. "I think this will cost you two chocolate bars."

"And one lollipop," Mama chimes in.

"Hey!" says Samir, walking into the room. He's wearing a new pair of Tommy Turtle trainers that Mama found in a shop. He stomps his foot now, and they light up. "Nobody is touching my Skittles!"

He looks so fierce that we all burst out laughing.

Milky Way Magazine

TELLING A TALE

by Farah Hajjar

Published in the Milky Way Literary Magazine, Issue 1

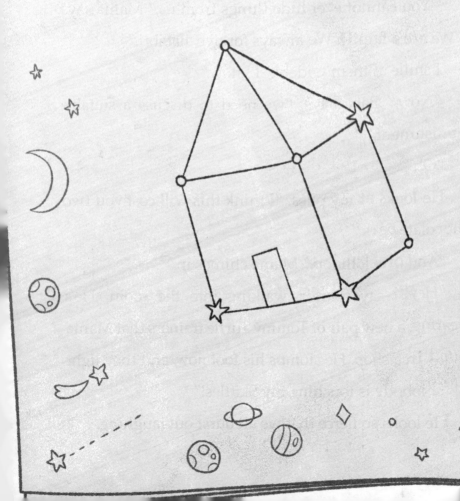

Issue #1

Once upon a time, there was a girl who was *usually* very clever, but sometimes she made bad decisions. Like the time she caused a fire in her house. It wasn't quite her fault. At least, there was nothing intentional about it. But it happened anyway.

The thing she did that wasn't clever was that she didn't tell anyone the truth.

Her parents were really stressed. Her little brother lost his favourite trainers and all his belongings. So she kept it a secret. She felt so awful about it, that a rock started to grow in her stomach. The rock got heavier and heavier until, one day, she couldn't get out of bed! She tried to stand up, but she fell down and rolled across the floor. In fact, she rolled right down the steps and out the front door and was never heard from again.

Farah's Writing Prompts

Sometimes, to write a story, you just need someone to give you an idea. The Milky Way creative writing club used several "starters" to get their members to be creative. These are called writing prompts. Here are a few of them to help you write your own stories.

- Write a story about a character who lives on a different planet. Give the planet a name and describe how its inhabitants look and how they live.

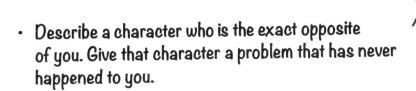

- Describe a character who is the exact opposite of you. Give that character a problem that has never happened to you.

- Imagine a character sitting in a room, reading a book or watching TV. Suddenly, another character bursts into the room and says, "You'll never believe what just happened! I was on my way home when ____." Who is the character? Finish his or her story.

- Write a story about a character who lives a life similar to yours and shares the same culture as you. It's your character's birthday, and he or she wakes up to find a giant box has been delivered to the front door. What's in it? Who sent it?

- Create a character who becomes invisible one day. What do people say when they think your character isn't around to hear it?

- Look in a dictionary and pick five random words. Then write a story using all of them.

- Who is your favourite fictional character from a book? Write a story in which you get to meet him or her.

Glossary

astrophysics science that has to do with objects in space and how they interact with one another

beige pale brown colour

douse throw water on

exaggerate make something seem bigger, better or more important than it really is

insurance contract between a person and a company to protect against damage or loss of valuable items

intentional done on purpose

labyrinth maze of winding passages that may be difficult to find the way out of

lectern stand with a slanted top, used to hold a book or papers

literary of or relating to books

nemesis opponent or enemy that is difficult to defeat

nitrogen colourless, odourless gas

orthoclase common white or pink mineral

petition letter that makes a request and is signed by many people

sarcastic using bitter or mocking words that are meant to hurt or make fun of someone or something

smoulder burn slowly with smoke but no flames

summarize give a shortened account of something using only the main points

thunderstruck greatly surprised

Glossary of Arabic Words

habibi my love (to a boy)

habibti my love (to a girl)

hajjar rocks

imshee walk

inshallah God willing, or I hope so

khalas enough

sana hilweh, ya gameel a sweet year for you (often used in a similar sense as and sung to the tune of "Happy Birthday")

warak dawali stuffed grape leaves

ABOUT THE AUTHOR

Susan Muaddi Darraj is an award-winning author of more than ten books, including two short story collections. She is an associate professor of English at Harford Community College in Bel Air, Maryland, USA, and she also teaches creative writing at Johns Hopkins University and Fairfield University. Susan loves books, coffee and baseball, and she's mildly obsessed with stationery supplies.

ABOUT THE ILLUSTRATOR

Illustrator and graphic designer Ruaida Mannaa completed her undergraduate studies at the Universidad del Norte in her hometown in Colombia. She went on to pursue a master's degree in illustration at the Savannah College of Art and Design in the United States. She grew up in a multicultural family, surrounded by different languages, loud parties and delicious food, and she finds great inspiration for her art in culture and cultural exchange.

Farah Rocks